shelve with Jewish Holiday books

DATE DUE

DEC 19 1990	JAN 05 2002		
DEC 23 1991	~~JAN 09 2010~~		
DEC 15 1992			
JAN 5 1993			
DEC 14 1993			
JAN 4 1994			
DEC 14 1994			
DEC 29 1994			
FEB 27 1995			
DEC 20 1995			
DEC 17 1998			
DEC 20 1999			

JAN 17 2004

HAPPY HANUKKAH REBUS

By David A. Adler

Illustrated by Jan Palmer

VIKING KESTREL

VIKING KESTREL
Published by the Penguin Group
Viking Penguin, a division of Penguin Books USA Inc.,
40 West 23rd Street, New York, New York 10010, U.S.A.
Penguin Books Ltd, 27 Wrights Lane, London W8 5TZ, England
Penguin Books Australia Ltd, Ringwood, Victoria, Australia
Penguin Books Canada Ltd, 2801 John Street, Markham, Ontario, Canada L3R 1B4
Penguin Books (N.Z.) Ltd, 182–190 Wairau Road, Auckland 10, New Zealand

Penguin Books Ltd, Registered Offices: Harmondsworth, Middlesex, England

First published in 1989 by Viking Penguin, a division of Penguin Books USA Inc.
Published simultaneously in Canada
1   3   5   7   9   10   8   6   4   2
Text copyright © David A. Adler, 1989
Illustrations copyright © Jan Palmer, 1989
All rights reserved

Library of Congress Cataloging-in-Publication Data
Adler, David A.   Happy Hanukkah rebus
David A. Adler ; pictures by Jan Palmer. p.   cm.
Summary: Sharon hears from her parents the story that underlies
their celebration of Hanukkah. In rebus format.
ISBN 0-670-82419-4
[1. Hanukkah—Fiction.   2. Rebuses.] I. Palmer, Jan, ill.   II. Title.
PZ7.A2612Hap   1989   [E]—dc20   89-8952

Printed in Japan.
Set in Bookman.

To Eitan Joshua with love

In *Happy Hanukkah Rebus,* many words or parts of words are replaced with pictures. A word written with pictures is called a rebus.

Some of the rebuses are easy to read. is house. is window. Other rebuses are more difficult. le is while. orah is menorah. EEE is armies.

If you have trouble reading some of the rebuses, check the glossary on page 29. The same story, without rebuses, begins on page 23. Have fun!

It was the 1ST 🌙 of Hanukkah. There were 3 Hanukkah 🧍orahs by the front 🪟 of Sharon's 🏠.

Sharon ⏱ed her 🍐ents put 🕯🕯 in the 🧍orahs.

Sharon & her 🍐ents said the blessings & lit the 🕯🕯. They sang Hanukkah songs. They played with the Hanukkah 🪀, the *dreidel*. Then they 8 🥔🥞.

Y le they 8 the 🥔🥞 Sharon's father said, "We 💡 the 🕯🕯, sing the songs, play dreidel, & eat 🥔🥞 2 remind us of the Hanukkah 🔍acles."

Sharon's mother said, "We 💡 the 🕯🕯 by the 🪟 so other 🧍acles will C them & will remember the 🔍acles, 2."

"More than 2000 y[ear] ago the Syrian [king] [ant]iochus tr[i]ed 2 4ce the Jews 2 give up th[eir] religion & 2 wor[ship] [eye] [idols]," Sharon's mother said. "A small group of Jewish [soldiers], the Macca[bees], fought the gr8 [arm]EEE of [ant]iochus & 1."

"Th[ere] was a [men]orah in the Temple with a [light] that always burned," Sharon's father said. "The Jews wanted re[light] the [men]orah. They found only enough oil 2 burn 1 day. But that oil burned 4 8 days until more oil could [bee] pre[pear]ed."

Sharon finished eating her [latkes]. "[I] must re-member the Hanukkah [mira]cles," Sharon said 2 herself.

🐝 **4** Sharon went **2** her room **2** play, she took **1** of the unlit Hanukkah 🕯🕯🕯. "This 🕯 will remind me of the Hanukkah miracles," Sharon said **2** herself.

Sharon's favorite 🎎 Anna🔔 was in a 🪑 n👂 the 🪟. Sharon put the 🕯 in Anna🔔's ✋ and 🐦ld her all about Hanukkah.

"If 👁 🇨 🇺 holding the 🕯 I will remember the Hanukkah 🪞cles," Sharon 🐦ld Anna🔔.

Then Sharon put her toy 🐕 Syl🧥er near Anna🔔's 🪑. "Syl🧥er will remind me **2** look at 🇺," Sharon 🐦ld Anna🔔, "& remember the Hanukkah 🪞cles."

Then Sharon set her toy 🚂 on the floor as if it were riding 2 ⛏ up Syl🪨er.

"This 🚂 will remind me 2 look at Syl🪨er & Syl🪨er will remind me 2 look at Anna🔔," Sharon said.

Then Sharon set 2 toy 🚗 on the floor as if they were riding 2 the 🚂.

"These 🚗 will remind me 2 look at the 🚂 & the 🚂 will remind me 2 look at Syl🪨er," Sharon said.

Then Sharon set a toy ⬤ & a toy ⬤ down 2 remind her 2 look at the ⬤. The —— of ⬤ & ⬤ ⬤ went in 2 the hall.

Sharon took a few of her small toy ⬤, a ⬤, a ⬤, a ⬤, 2 ⬤, & 4 ⬤ & set them in a —— ⬤hind the ⬤ & ⬤ ⬤.

Sharon put 4 ⬤ on the floor ⬤hind the last ⬤ 2 remind her 2 look at the ⬤.

Sharon set a ⬤le of ⬤ on the floor ⬤hind the ⬤. She put a few ⬤ on the floor ⬤hind the ⬤ & her toy ⬤ ⬤hind the ⬤.

"Sharon," her father called. "It's 👔 me 2 get E 4 🛏."

Sharon's 🍐 ents came upstairs & 🪚 of the toy ☎, the 🧸🧸, the 🧱, the 📚, the 🐎🐎, 🐘🐘, 🦒, 🐯, & 🦁 on the floor. They 🪚 the 🚗 & 🚛, the 🚂, the 🐕 & the 👧 sitting in the 🪑.

"Y R all these 🏀🐴 on the floor?" Sharon's mother asked.

Sharon looked at Syl[vest]er, the [train] , the [car] & [truck] [truck] , the [fox] , [books] , [blocks] , [dolls] , & toy [telephone] . She looked at Anna [bell] .

"[eye] put them all here 2 remind me of $+\frac{2}{2}{4}$ thing," Sharon said.

"2 remind [U] of what?" her [pear]ents asked.

Sharon looked at all the [horse] , but she could [knot] re-member about the Hanukkah [mirror]cles.

"[eye] [4]got," she [told] her [pear]ents.

19

Sharon got E 4 🛏. Her 🍐ents helped her 2 put away her 🐴. But they left Anna 🔔 in her n👂 the 🪟. The Hanukkah 🕯 was still in her ✋.

Sharon's father said, "👁 M sure that 2morrow U will remember Y U put all the 🐴 on the floor."

Then Sharon's mother said, "Good 🌙 & ha P Ha-nukkah."

The Story Without Rebuses

It was the first night of Hanukkah. There were three Hanukkah menorahs by the front window of Sharon's house. Sharon watched her parents put candles in the menorahs.

Sharon and her parents said the blessings and lit the candles. They sang Hanukkah songs. They played with the Hanukkah top, the *dreidel*. Then they ate potato pancakes.

While they ate the potato pancakes Sharon's father said, "We light the candles, sing the songs, play dreidel, and eat potato pancakes to remind us of the Hanukkah miracles."

Sharon's mother said, "We light the candles by the window so other people will see them and will remember the miracles, too."

"More than two thousand years ago, the Syrian king Antiochus tried to force the Jews to give up their religion and to worship idols," Sharon's mother said. "A small group of Jewish soldiers, the Maccabees, fought the great armies of Antiochus and won."

"There was a menorah in the Temple with a light that always burned," Sharon's father said. "The Jews wanted to relight the menorah. They found only enough oil to burn one day. But that oil burned for eight days until more oil could be prepared."

Sharon finished eating her potato pancakes. "I must remember the Hanukkah miracles," Sharon said to herself.

Before Sharon went to her room to play, she took one of the unlit Hanukkah candles. "This candle will remind me of the Hanukkah miracles," Sharon said to herself.

Sharon's favorite doll Annabel was in a chair near the window. Sharon put the candle in Annabel's hand and told her all about Hanukkah.

"If I see you holding the candle I will remember the Hanukkah miracles," Sharon told Annabel.

Then Sharon put her toy dog Sylvester near Annabel's chair. "Sylvester will remind me to look at you," Sharon told Annabel, "and remember the Hanukkah miracles."

Then Sharon set her toy train on the floor as if it were riding to pick up Sylvester.

"This train will remind me to look at Sylvester and Sylvester will remind me to look at Annabel," Sharon said.

Then Sharon set two toy cars on the floor as if they were riding to the train.

"These cars will remind me to look at the train and the train will remind me to look at Sylvester." Sharon said.

Then Sharon set a toy red fire engine and a toy oil truck down to remind her to look at the cars. The line of cars and trucks went into the hall.

Sharon took a few of her small toy animals, a lion, a tiger, a giraffe, two elephants, and four horses and set them in a line behind the cars and trucks.

Sharon put four books on the floor behind the last horse to remind her to look at the animals.

Sharon set a pile of blocks on the floor behind the books. She put a few puppets on the floor behind the blocks and her toy telephone behind the puppets.

"Sharon," her father called. "It's time to get ready for bed."

Sharon's parents came upstairs and saw the toy telephone, the puppets, the blocks, the books, the horses, elephants, giraffe, tiger, and lion on the floor. They saw the cars and trucks, the train, the dog and the doll sitting in the chair.

"Why are all these toys on the floor?" Sharon's mother asked.

Sharon looked at Sylvester, the train, the cars and trucks, the animals, books, blocks, puppets, and toy telephone. She looked at Annabel.

"I put them all here to remind me of something," Sharon said.

"To remind you of what?" her parents asked.

Sharon looked at all the toys, but she could not remember about the Hanukkah miracles.

"I forgot," she told her parents.

Sharon got ready for bed. Her parents helped her to put away her toys. But they left Annabel in her chair near the window. The Hanukkah candle was still in her hand.

Sharon's father said, "I am sure that tomorrow you will remember why you put all the toys on the floor."

Then Sharon's mother said, "Good night and happy Hanukkah."

GLOSSARY

The rebuses in this glossary are in the order that they first appear in the story.

1ST	first	&	and
🌙	night	🪀	top
3	three	**8**	ate, eight
👥orah	menorah	🥔	potato
🪟	window	🥞	pancakes
🏠	house	**Y**le	while
⏱ed	watched	💡	light
🍐ents	parents	**2**	to, too, two
🕯🕯🕯	candles	🪞cles	miracles

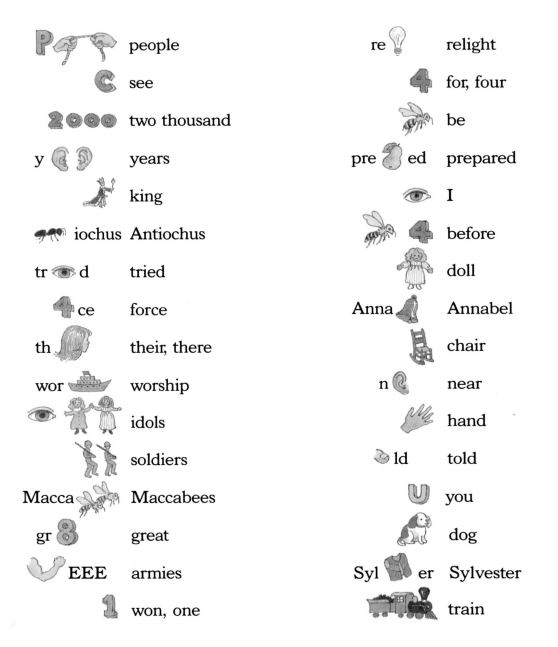

P	people	re	relight
C	see	4	for, four
2000	two thousand	(bee)	be
y (ears)	years	pre (pear) ed	prepared
(king)	king	(eye)	I
(ant) iochus	Antiochus	(bee) 4	before
tr (eye) d	tried	(doll)	doll
4 ce	force	Anna (bell)	Annabel
th (hair)	their, there	(chair)	chair
wor (ship)	worship	n (ear)	near
(eye)(idols)	idols	(hand)	hand
(soldiers)	soldiers	(toe) ld	told
Macca (bees)	Maccabees	U	you
gr 8	great	(dog)	dog
(arm) EEE	armies	Syl (vest) er	Sylvester
1	won, one	(train)	train

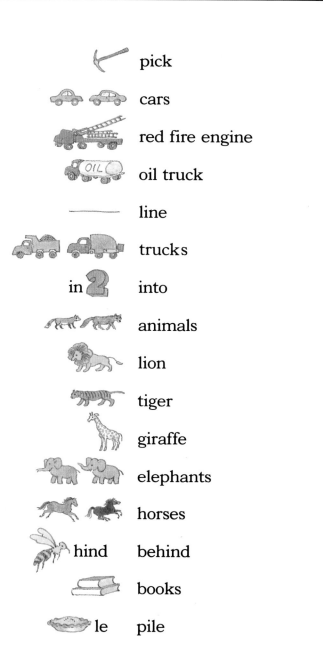

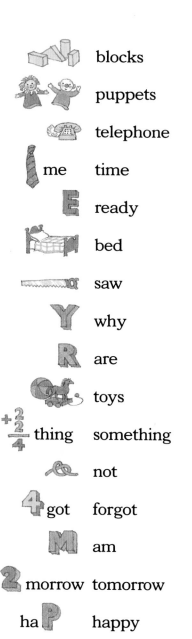

pick

cars

red fire engine

oil truck

line

trucks

in 2   into

animals

lion

tiger

giraffe

elephants

horses

hind   behind

books

le   pile

blocks

puppets

telephone

me   time

ready

bed

saw

why

are

toys

thing   something

not

got   forgot

am

morrow   tomorrow

ha P   happy